P9-CFG-436

GOOD NIGHT, ORANGE MONSTER

GOOD NIGHT, ORANGE MONSTER

Betty Jean Lifton

Illustrated by Cyndy Szekeres

Atheneum   1972   New York

For Ken and Karen,
        who shared the Orange Monster,
even though
        they didn't share the closet.

GOOD NIGHT, ORANGE MONSTER

1

There was once a little boy named Ken who was very clever. He could skate on one blade. He could catch a ball and even hit one with a bat—sometimes. He could bait his own hook and fish from a pier. He could catch butterflies in a net, fireflies in a jar and frogs with his bare hands. But he had one problem. He was afraid of monsters.

At night when Ken's mother tucked him into bed, he would say, "Mother, I want another glass of water!" Or "I want another story!" Or "I want another light on!" And when all else had failed, he would shout, "Mother, Mother, there's a monster!"

"Nonsense," his mother would reply. "There's no such thing as monsters."

"But I heard one."

"Where?"

"In the closet."

"There's nothing in the closet but clothes and toys," his mother would say patiently. "Now go to sleep."

And finally when he was so full of water he could have floated like a balloon into the night sky, he would bury his head under the covers and fall asleep.

2

Now the truth is that Ken was right. There was a monster who lived in his closet. He was a small monster, no larger than Ken. His name was Moogi, and he stayed there all alone with his mother. His father was outside in a dark, dank cave where big monsters belong.

You see, monsters like to raise their children in closets until they grow up. Closets are warmer than drafty caves, and are filled with so many nice things. Beautiful clothes to wear, belts to swing on, shelves to sleep on and—most important—wonderful toys to play with.

Of course, living in someone else's closet has it disadvantages too. Moogi had to change all the games so that he could use them. For example, Monster Monopoly is much different from ordinary Monopoly. Instead of landing on streets with names like Broadway or Atlantic Avenue, you land on Spook Street or Ghost Alley. And instead of building ordinary houses and hotels, you build haunted ones.

Then too, Kings and Queens and Jokers on playing cards must be changed to goblins, witches and vampires. ABC books must be changed from A is for Apple to A is for Attic, B is for Ball to B is for Bat, C is for Cat to C is for Closet. And even M is for Mother must be made to read M is for Monster.

But although Moogi had everything a little monster could want in the closet, he had one problem. He was afraid of little boys.

In the morning when his mother tucked him into his shelf—for monsters are up and about at night when you are sleeping, and when you get up, they are ready for bed—he would cry, "Mother, I want another ghost story!" Or "I want another mug of monster milk!"

And when all else had failed, he would shout, "Mother, I'm afraid!"

"Afraid of what?" his mother would ask.

"Something will get me."

"Now what could possibly get you?"

"A boy. I'm afraid of boys."

"Nonsense. There is no such thing as boys."

"But I heard one outside the closet."

"Must have been something harmless like a rat or bat," his mother would reassure him. And she would sit by his side weaving a quilt of spider-web thread that would someday cover him in the cave, until he fell asleep.

3

One night in the bedroom Ken could not sleep. He tried every position he could think of, even his feet on the pillow, but nothing worked. Then he thought he heard a noise in the closet. Like a block falling. He knew his mother would be angry if he called her again, so he decided to get up and open the closet door just a crack.

Very softly he turned the knob and peeked in.

Now at that very moment the little monster had tip-toed to the door too, and they were both there at the same time. Their startled eyes met. Their noses almost touched. Then Ken slammed the door and went screaming back to his bed and Moogi went screaming to his shelf.

"Mother, Mother, I saw a monster!" cried Ken.

"Nonsense," she said. "I told you there is no such a thing as monsters." And since she was a grown-up, she believed this to be true.

But Ken knew for sure there were such things as monsters. He had seen one.

And Moogi knew there were such things as boys. He had seen one.

And though they never would have admitted it to anyone—even to themselves—each had liked what he had seen.

4

It was a week before Christmas and the whole house—inside the closet and out—was full of holiday cheer. The closet was especially cheerful, for Ken's mother was hiding his presents there. It was the one place she knew he wouldn't dare look.

Moogi was having a marvellous time playing with each new toy as it arrived. And Moogi's mother had found a way to rewrap the packages so that no one would know they had ever been opened.

The present the little monster liked best was the Monster–Making–Machine. It came with molds and colored liquids that could make terrible monsters with sharp claws and hideous fangs. The scarier the better as far as Moogi was concerned.

Moogi attached the machine to the plug right by his shelf. Sometimes black fumes filled the closet so completely that Moogi's mother could not see to weave her spider-web quilt.

"I don't mind fire," she would say, "but this smoke is too much. Why don't you draw some goblins with those new crayons or mold some vampires out of clay?"

But Moogi only wanted to make monsters on his Monster–Making–Machine.

On Christmas day Ken opened all his presents under the tree. There were so many things, each more marvellous than the other, but the one he liked best was the Monster–Making–Machine. He took it up to his room and made monsters from early in the morning until late in the afternoon.

"Why don't you go out on your new sled?" his mother kept saying.

"Why don't you play with your electric trains?" his father asked more than once.

"I still have more monsters to do," Ken would reply. He was really trying to make a monster just like the one he had seen in his closet, but each one either came out too fat, too thin or too lopsided. He just couldn't get the one he wanted.

"Then at least open a window," his mother said at last. "This room is full of smoke."

But Ken didn't mind the smoke at all.

That night he lined all his little monsters up by the machine on the small table next to his bed.

"This is the best Christmas I ever had," he mumbled as he fell asleep.

5

When Moogi awoke that same evening, he put on Ken's new cowboy jacket and started for the Monster–Making–Machine. But it wasn't there. Where could it have gone so suddenly? He would have cried, but he knew that monsters, no matter how young, do not have tears.

Then, opening the closet door a crack, he spotted his beloved machine next to the boy's bed. Even his fear of boys could not keep him from rushing over to it.

Very quietly Moogi plugged the machine in right where it was, and continued making more monsters. He was having such a good time he didn't notice that the smoke was curling over Ken's head like a dark cloud.

Ken gave a short snort in his sleep and then sat up with a cough. He couldn't believe his eyes. There was the little monster wearing *his* cowboy jacket, sitting in *his* chair and using *his* Monster machine. He was so surprised he could not even call out for his mother.

Finally, he said as bravely as he could, "I beg your pardon, that is *my* machine."

Moogi's heart beat rapidly under Ken's jacket (for when they are little, monsters do have hearts), but he just continued working on an orange monster he had almost finished. "It is *my* machine," he replied at last.

"But I got it for Christmas today," argued Ken.

"I got it a week ago," said Moogi, giving the orange monster his final fang.

Ken did not know what to say to that.

"You are a monster, aren't you?" he asked after a few moments of smoke-filled silence.

"Of course," said Moogi proudly. "And you're a boy, aren't you?"

"Of course," said Ken, and now he was proud, too. And curious. "Are you related to Bat Man or Dracula?"

"Never heard of them," said Moogi, adding, "Would you like to make some monsters with me?"

"Oh, yes," said Ken eagerly.

And soon the two of them were hard at work creating the most ferocious monsters you have ever seen. Even Moogi was secretly afraid of them. Besides the orange one, there were gray ones, brown ones, purple ones, green ones and some silver ones that shone in the dark. Some had pointed heads and some had round heads; and some had no heads at all. Ken and his new friend might have continued making them until dawn if the colored liquid for the molds hadn't run out.

"I'll get some more tomorrow," promised Ken.

"Then I'll be back tomorrow night," said Moogi. "And let's make some boys to go with the monsters."

"Great idea," said Ken. "Boys can be scary too."

"I know," said the little monster.

And the closet door closed with a weird click that no grown-up could ever hear.

6

Moogi's mother was amazed at how quickly her son went to bed that morning. There was no dawdling on his way to the shelf. He didn't ask for another ghost story or more monster milk. In fact, he didn't even say he was afraid of boys.

"Are you feeling all right?" she asked.

"Fine."

"Maybe the closet isn't drafty enough for you."

"It's just right."

"Maybe you're lonely without other monsters to play with."

"No."

"There'd be more to do out in the cave."

"I like it here." And Moogi closed his eyes and pretended to be asleep.

"Could it be that my little monster is growing up?" wondered his mother as she wove away on her spiderweb quilt. "Could it be that he is old enough for the cave?"

7

Ken's mother was also amazed at how easily her son went to bed that night. He could hardly wait until supper was over. Then he rushed upstairs, got into his pajamas by himself, brushed his teeth without being told and jumped under the covers.

"Are you ill?" asked his mother.

"No, just sleepy."

"Would you like a story?"

"No, thanks, not tonight."

"Some water?"

"I'm not thirsty."

"Well, good night. . . ."

"Good night. And Mother. . . ."

"Yes?"

"You can turn off my light. I want it to be dark in here tonight.

His mother went downstairs shaking her head in disbelief. "The Christmas excitement must have been too much for him," she told Ken's father. "But he doesn't seem to have a fever."

"Maybe something he ate," said Ken's father from behind his newspaper.

8

As soon as his mother was gone, Ken dashed over to
the closet and gave a little rap. Moogi opened the door
right away before *his* mother could hear. And then
they went to work making boys on the Monster–
Making–Machine.

They made the most scary boys you could imagine. Some had horns, some claws, some bat-like wings, some had three eyes and one had two heads. They came in all colors too—dark purple, blood-red, mud-brown and silver-gray. There was one that was as pink as a cow's tongue and another as blue as the bottom of the sea.

"Blue is my favorite color," said Ken.

"Then this blue boy is my favorite," said Moogi. "I'll keep it to remember you by."

"And I'll keep this orange monster you were making last night to remember you by," said Ken.

"Goodnight, Blue Boy," said Orange Monster.

"Goodnight, Orange Monster," said Blue Boy.

And they did not know, neither monsters nor boys, that this was the last time they would all be together.

9

That same night, while Ken slept, Moogi's father suddenly appeared in the closet.

"I hear you're growing up," he bellowed. "So it's time to move into the cave."

"Not yet," cried Moogi.

"You can't spend the rest of your life in a closet," grunted his father.

"Why not?"

"It's not done by respectable monsters," roared his father. "You must go forth into dark woods and deserted castles."

While his mother was busy packing up the spider-web quilt and fixing the closet so that no one would know they had ever been there, Moogi went forth into Ken's bedroom. He wanted to waken his friend to tell him he was going, but he knew monsters do not say goodbye—they just disappear.

So instead he placed his collection of monsters and boys on the table there—except for Blue Boy, whom he was taking with him.

He hoped Ken would understand.

10

And when Ken woke the next morning and saw that Moogi had left everything except Blue Boy, he did understand. He put Moogi's monsters and boys together with his own monsters and boys in an old shoe box where he used to keep his marbles. Only Orange Monster was left out on the table.

All that day he was very quiet. That night he again refused a story, a glass of water or a light on. And for the first time he told his mother she could open his closet door.

"But your monster!" exclaimed his mother, getting more and more confused.

"He isn't in there anymore," replied Ken simply.

"Where did he go?"

"He grew up and went out with his family."

"How do you know?"

"I guess I'm growing up too," said Ken.

"Well, don't grow up too fast," cried his mother. "Have a glass of water, please. For my sake."

"All right, if it makes you happy."

It did.

Then his mother opened the closet door as he had asked, and tiptoed out.

"Good night, Orange Monster," whispered Ken into the darkness.

Perhaps it was the wind—but he thought he heard a familiar voice from far off call, "Good night, Blue Boy."

And he fell asleep.